The Railway Cat and the Ghost

The Railway Cat and the Ghost

Phyllis Arkle

Illustrated by Stephanie Hawken

Hodder Children's Books

a division of Hodder Headline plc

A Catalogue record for this book is available from the
British Library

ISBN 0 340 69993 0

Typeset by Avon Dataset Ltd, Bidford-on-Avon, Warks

Printed and bound in Great Britain by
Caledonian International Book Manufacturing Ltd, Glasgow

Hodder and Stoughton
A division of Hodder Headline PLC
338 Euston Road
London NW1 3BH

Contents

1   The Chocolate Cat   1
2   A Snake at the Station   11
3   The Ghost at Hilltop
    Farm   21
4   Alfie the Train Driver   31
5   Diamond Rescue   39
6   Zara The Fortune
    Teller   49

1

The Chocolate Cat

It was early morning. Alfie the Railway Cat was feeling very sorry for himself as he waited for Fred, the Leading Chargeman, to come on duty.

Poor Alfie was covered from the tops of his ears to the tip of his tail in brown paint. There had been an accident. Alfie knew that Ginger his friend from the station, hadn't meant to knock a tin of paint off the ledge, but Alfie had been sitting just underneath. Now he felt sticky and miserable.

Soon Alfie saw Fred approaching. Fred was

Alfie's best friend, though he was fond of Brown, too. But he couldn't stand Hack, the Leading Railman, and was glad that Hack was late on duty today. Alfie didn't want mean old Hack seeing him in such a sorry state.

'Miaow! Miaow! Miaow!' Alfie called to Fred. *Help! Help! Help!*

'Hello, there,' said Fred, cheerfully, when he was in earshot.

'Haven't seen *you* before. Can't have two cats chasing one another up and down the platforms.'

'Miaow! Miaow! Miaow!' said Alfie again. *I'm your Alfie.*

He managed to stagger to his feet and rub his chin against Fred's trouser leg, but he felt so heavy he fell back again, exhausted.

Fred looked puzzled. 'What's the matter, old chap,' he asked. 'If our Alfie has been causing trouble I'll let him have the sharp edge of my tongue and no fish for at least a week.'

'Miaow!' moaned Alfie. '*It's me here.*'

Fred bent down and put out his hand. And Alfie pretended to bite his thumb.

'That's just what Alfie does!' exclaimed Fred. 'How do *you* know . . . ? He took a good long look at Alfie before starting to stroke him again. Immediately his hand sprang away. It was sticky.

'Paint!' he shouted. 'You poor Alfie. However did you—?'

Just then Brown arrived.

'Ever seen this cat before?' cried Fred.

'No,' said Brown, glancing at Alfie.

'Miaow!' said Alfie. What a lie!

'Take a closer look,' urged Fred. Brown stared at Alfie.

'Well, well, well,' he said, amazed. 'I do believe – no, no, it can't possibly be our Alfie – but I'd recognise that face anywhere.'

Fred nodded.

'But who is responsible for this outrage?' Brown asked indignantly.

'Well, my guess is as good as yours,' replied Fred. 'But it wouldn't surprise me if the workmen left an open tin of paint somewhere, and Alfie and Ginger have been larking about with it?'

'Could be,' said Brown.

'Ring the vet straight away. Tell him it's urgent. The paint will start to harden if it's left any longer and we'll have a job to remove it then. The first commuters will be arriving soon. Any sign of Hack?'

'No,' said Brown as he ran out of the office.

'Always late, that Hack,' grumbled Fred. He gently scooped Alfie up and, holding him at arms length, carried him into the office.

Soon Alfie was lying on a towel on top of Fred's desk.

Brown came in. 'Vet's coming straight away,' he reported.

'Not a word about this to Hack,' said Fred. Alfie wouldn't want to be seen in his present state.'

'MIAOW!' howled Alfie. I would *not*. Off went Brown to attend to passengers and soon Hack appeared in the doorway.

'Late again!' shouted Fred. 'I'm tired of warning you. This time I've decided to cut your wages by half to compensate the company for hours lost.' He moved to stand in front of Alfie.

'Oh, come off it, Fred,' said Hack, his hands in his pockets. 'Only ten minutes late . . .'

'*Fifteen* minutes,' Fred said glancing at the clock. 'Get moving, or else . . .'

As Hack turned to go he caught a glimpse of Alfie. 'What a beautiful cat,' he said. 'Lovely chocolate colour. Who's the owner?'

Fred shook his head.

But Hack hadn't finished. 'Let's get rid of Alfie and keep this cat instead.'

'Get rid of Alfie?' cried Fred. 'What a good idea! Peace at last,' he said. 'I won't have to put up with you two quarrelling all the time.'

Hack looked taken aback. 'Well ... er ... I don't know ...' he began uneasily. 'Perhaps we had better keep Alfie for a ...'

'No, no,' said Fred, firmly. 'Now is our chance to get rid of poor old Alfie.'

'Miaow! Miaow! Miaow!' protested Alfie weakly. I'm not poor and I'm not very old either.

'Are you listening, Hack?' said Fred. If you do not get on to that platform immediately, Mrs Hack can have you at home all day, with no pay. OUT! OUT! OUT! QUICK MARCH!' Hack rushed out and Fred grinned at Alfie.

'We'll get the better of him one day, Alfie. You'll see,' he said.

Brown returned. 'Any sign of the vet?' he asked.

'Not yet,' said Fred. 'Now listen, Brown. Keep an eye on Hack. Tell him nothing about Alfie, or the vet. I don't want him here until Alfie has been restored to his old self.'

'Right,' said Mr Brown, on his way out.

The vet arrived. 'I smell paint,' he said, staring at Alfie. 'And I think I know who is underneath that smelly stuff.'

'Miaow!' said Alfie, glad that someone had recognised him.

'Been fighting?' asked the vet.

'Miaow!' cried Alfie. Not *really* fighting.

The vet began to examine Alfie as Fred looked on anxiously.

'Fortunately the paint is not very thick,' said the vet. 'I'll soon get if off with a special liquid. Just be patient and keep still, Alfie.'

'Miaow!' said Alfie. Anything you say. He managed to keep still while the vet carefully wiped his fur until every speck of paint had disappeared.

'Excellent. Alfie looks as good as new,' said Fred.

And Alfie said 'Miaow.' Thank you. A hundred times.

'Cup of coffee?' suggested Fred.

'No, thank you,' said the vet. 'Farmer Marsh's pony needs attention. I must be on my way, but I'll look in tomorrow morning to make quite sure Alfie has recovered from his ordeal. See he keeps out of trouble. Bye.'

Brown ran in to make sure Alfie was back to normal. 'Oh! Just look at him,' he cried. 'He's as good as new and as handsome as ever.'

'You'd better get back to the Booking Office,' Fred told him. Adding, with a wink,

'Send Hack in to see me.'

Hack strolled in a few minutes later.

'Quick! Quick march!' shouted Fred.

Hack made an effort and nearly fell over. As he straightened up he noticed Alfie, nibbling a tasty piece of cod that Fred's wife had sent for him.

'What's *he* doing in here? asked Hack.

'He lives here,' said Fred sarcastically.

'Yes, yes, I know he does, but where's that beautiful cat I saw earlier on?'

'Glad you confess at last that Alfie's beautiful,' said Fred, grinning at Brown who

was peeping round the door.

'No *not* Alfie,' said Hack. 'I mean that lovely chocolate-coloured cat I saw sitting on the desk.'

Brown came in and Fred said, 'Have *you* seen a beautiful brown cat in here?'

'No,' said Brown. 'Only Alfie has been in here all morning. I can vouch for that.'

'But . . . but I *saw* it with my very own eyes,' cried Hack.

Fred patted him on the shoulder. 'Sit down and compose yourself for a minute, he said, adding, 'Have you been getting enough sleep.'

'Yes, yes, I have,' shouted Hack.

'Well calm down,' said Fred. 'We've a busy day ahead.'

Unable to control his mirth any longer, Brown rushed out and Fred followed.

Alfie looked at Hack. 'Miaow!' he said. Take no notice of them. They think it's funny.

Alfie thought it was funny, too – not the paint part, of course – but he felt a little bit sorry for Hack. To keep in Fred's good books he decided to avoid confrontation with Hack as much as possible – at least for one week – or perhaps one day would be enough?

2

A Snake at the Station

Alfie was in no hurry to have breakfast the next morning, for it was Hack's turn to bring fish for him. The fish would be cooked by Mrs Hack, who in Alfie's opinion was no cook. Her fish was either underdone or burnt.

When Hack appeared carrying a very large newspaper parcel, Alfie was still half asleep in his basket.

'Get up!' shouted Hack. 'Lazy, lazy bones!' Alfie ignored him, but he did wonder if his breakfast was in that large parcel.

'Oh I see,' said Hack. 'Awkward as usual.

Well, two can play at that game. When your highness *does* want breakfast he can search for it. I am going to hide it.' And off he went.

'Miaow!' replied Alfie. Fancy wanting to play Hide and Seek at your age.

A little while later Alfie sat up, scratched his head with his left hind foot and flopped down again for half an hour or so. Then he decided that he *was* hungry. He would have to put up with Mrs Hack's offering. He jumped out of the basket and gave himself a quick lick or two before joining Hack and a few waiting passengers. He looked up at Hack. 'Miaow!' he cried. 'I'm ready for breakfast.'

Hack took no notice, so Alfie continued to protest loudly. A passenger spoke up. 'What's the matter with Alfie?' he asked. 'Has he had breakfast?'

Hack shook his head.

'Well give it to him,' said the man, 'or I'll report you for neglecting a famous cat.'

'Miaow!' purred Alfie. Thank you.

Hack shrugged his shoulders and Alfie followed him to the parcels office. Hack opened the door. 'Your breakfast is in here,' he said, with what Alfie thought was a nasty grin. 'I'll leave the door open.'

With some misgivings, Alfie entered the parcels office. He sniffed among the parcels waiting for collection or delivery, and jumped up onto the shelves. He even looked into the wastepaper bin, but he could find no trace of the newspaper parcel.

Then he noticed something he had overlooked. The door of a large cupboard under the counter was open slightly. He put a front paw into the gap and managed to prise the door open. He poked his head into the

cupboard and saw a crumpled newspaper – and something else as well. Something large, curled up, greyish-green, with black and orange markings, glittering eyes and a forked tongue hanging out of its mouth.

'Miaow! Miaow! MIAOW! MIAOW!' howled Alfie in fright. He dashed out of the room.

Fred came running and picked him up. 'Whatever is the matter, Alfie?' he cried anxiously as Alfie, trembling all over, dug his front paws in Fred's jacket.

People ran up wanting to know what was going on. 'Don't know,' said Fred. 'It's not like Alfie to make such a fuss.'

'I saw him dash out of the parcels office,' said a woman.

'Well,' said Fred. 'I'll go and have a look around for anything unusual.' He handed Alfie to the woman.

'Oh dear, do be careful,' she begged. 'There may be a wild animal inside there.'

Fred started to make a thorough search and soon noticed the open cupboard door. He peered inside and fell back, gasping at what he saw. He ran out of the room, the door banging behind him, shouting, 'No panic! No panic! Send for the police and the vet!'

Brown was already on his way to the phone and Fred managed to blurt out, 'It's . . . it's . . . it's a snake, a great big hideous snake with evil, glittering eyes.' He shuddered and gasped. 'A mon . . . mon . . . MONSTER!'

Hack started to back away, but Fred ordered, 'Stay where you are. You may be needed.'

A policeman arrived and Fred, his voice still trembling, managed to tell him about the great big hideous snake with awful glittering eyes.

'A *snake*? Are you sure?' asked the policeman.

'Yes, yes,' Fred assured him, 'a great big, fat, hideous . . .'

'All right. All right. Calm down,' said the policeman. I'll have to go and see for myself.'

'Oh, don't go in alone, please,' begged the woman nervously, clutching Alfie so tightly he could hardly breathe.

'Don't worry,' the policeman assured her. 'I'll take a quick look – and a quick exit if necessary.'

No one spoke, and soon the policeman's voice was heard. 'There *is* something here. What on earth . . . ?'

There was silence for a couple of minutes and then the officer emerged. The waiting group stepped back in horror. For around his neck was a great bloated snake, with enormous glittering eyes.

'He's being throttled by the snake,' yelled Brown. 'Send for the police, an ambulance, an . . .'

'Calm down,' cried the policeman. 'Stay where you are. This is no snake. It's an old bicycle tyre, slightly inflated and painted.'

'But what about those awful glittering eyes?' asked Fred.

'Glass buttons, glued on,' was the reply. 'Has anyone any idea who is responsible for this stupid prank?'

'I think I know . . .' began Fred.

But Hack interrupted. 'Well, er . . . er . . . It was only a joke to frighten Alfie,' he said. 'That cat's a menace.'

'Well, I'll give *you* the fright of your life before the day's out.' said Fred.

'And I'll report you for wasting police time,' shouted the policeman as he strode out of the station, with the 'snake' still coiled around his neck.

Fred turned to Hack. 'From now on, you will treat Alfie with the greatest respect and for the next four weeks you will bring him a tail-end of fresh salmon, which must be cooked to perfection by Mrs Hack. Understand?'

Hack shuffled his feet and nodded.

Alfie was already looking forward to the Salmon, but wished Fred would ask someone else to do the cooking.

3

The Ghost at Hill Top Farm

Alfie needed a holiday. It wasn't fair. All the station cats except himself had holidays. He decided he would go and stay at Hill Top Farm for a week. Mr Jones, the farmer, and his wife – and Bryn the dog – always made him very welcome and the other farm animals all liked Alfie. They were used to his regular visits to the farm.

Alfie didn't waste any time. The next morning he set off for the small farm on top of a hill, just half a mile from the station. When he arrived, Alfie joined Spot, the farm cat, outside the kitchen door and together they started miaowing – We want breakfast! We want breakfast!

Mrs Jones opened the door, and Bryn rushed out barking a welcome to Alfie. The two cats dashed in and sat down by the pantry door.

'I suppose you've come for breakfast, Alfie,' said Mrs Jones. 'Have they run out of food at the station?'

'Miaow!' sang Alfie. I've come for a week's holiday, with full board and lodging please.

The farmer came running down the stairs. 'Well, well, well, you are a welcome visitor, Alfie,' he cried. 'You can help Spot get rid of the rats and mice we've got here. They're a right menace at present.'

'Miaow!' said Alfie. I'm good at dealing with pests.

Meanwhile, back at the station, Fred was having similar trouble with unwanted rats and mice. 'That cat's gone off again – just when he's needed.'

'Can't think why you keep him,' muttered Hack. 'He's a nuisance, a mischief maker, a stupid—'

'That's enough from you, thank you,' said Fred sharply. 'I wouldn't be surprised if Alfie has gone up to Hill Top Farm to get away from you and your snide comments, but we *do* need him here. Go and bring him back.'

Hack opened his mouth to protest but Fred was firm. 'Go, *now*,' he ordered.

Muttering to himself, Hack set off for the farm to fetch Alfie.

By a stroke of luck, Alfie saw Hack climbing up the hill. He quickly scrambled up a tree trunk and hid amongst the leaves.

Hack banged on the kitchen door until Mrs

Jones appeared. 'And what do *you* want?' she asked.

'I've come for that wretch, Alfie. He is needed back at the station.'

'Well take him then,' said Mrs Jones.

'Where is he?' said Hack.

Mrs Jones was a busy woman. She stared at him. 'Do you *really* expect me to know where Alfie is? Go and search for yourself.'

'But . . .' began Hack.

Mrs Jones shut the door on him.

Alfie settled down in the tree. He watched as Hack trudged around the farm, calling out 'Alfie! Alfie!' Sometimes adding, 'I'll get you for this!'

Flicker the pony snorted at Hack and the six sheep bleated, while Bryn padded gently behind him.

Eventually Hack gave up the search and returned to the station.

Fred was furious. 'What do you mean, you can't find him?' he roared. 'Well, each day after you have signed off duty you will go up to the farm and search for Alfie – even if it takes twelve months or more to find him.'

'But it will be dark by the time I get to the farm,' Hack moaned. 'I'll never find him.'

'Oh yes you will. It will be suppertime and Alfie won't be far from the kitchen,' said Fred.

Fred was right. Alfie was full and comfortable in the farmhouse kitchen when Hack knocked on the door. Guessing who it might be, Alfie squeezed underneath Mr Jones's fireside chair. He lay as still as a mouse.

'I've been searching high and low for that crafty cat of ours,' said Hack. 'Is he in your kitchen by any chance?'

Mr Jones flung wide the door. 'I can't see him, can you?'

'Oh, come on,' cried Hack. We need Alfie at the station. Perhaps he's upstairs?'

Cats are not allowed in the bedrooms,' said the farmer. 'Sorry, but you'll have to look somewhere else. Goodnight.'

Hack appeared at the farm the next night, and the one after that.

Mrs Jones had had enough of him. 'We'll keep Alfie here until the weekend,' she said to her husband. 'But we'll have to stop Hack coming to look for him every evening. Any ideas?'

The farmer thought for a minute or two, then he smiled. 'I've got a good idea,' he said. 'Hack said he was on late duty tomorrow. That means it will be nearly midnight before he comes looking for Alfie. We'll get the ghost to frighten him off.'

'But we haven't got a ghost,' said Mrs Jones.

'Oh, but we have. Flicker can dress up in those old white curtains that are waiting for the wash. He will be the Horse Ghost.'

Mrs Jones laughed. 'But how—?' she began.

'Easy,' was the reply. 'Flicker will love it. Drape one curtain over his back and the other over his head and shoulders. I'll make a white paper mask with holes for his eyes and ears and we'll hang a lantern round his neck to light up his eyes.'

Mrs Jones laughed. 'I don't know . . .' she began.

'Hack won't even have to climb up the hill. Flicker will go rushing to welcome him as he always does,' said Mr Jones. 'What do you think, Alfie?'

'Miaow!' cried Alfie. Very funny, but I hope Hack won't be too frightened.

Early the next evening, Alfie and Spot watched Flicker being dressed for the haunting. The horse was obviously enjoying all the attention but he soon grew restless.

'He's telling us it's time for Hack's arrival,' said Mrs Jones.

'There's no moon out tonight,' said Mr Jones 'and Hack's coming.'

Sure enough, a light from Hack's torch could be seen as he climbed the hill. Mr Jones quickly released Flicker, who trotted down the hill to meet the Railman. Hack glanced up and stood terror-stricken, as the ghostly

apparition galloped towards him.

'Aaaagh! Aaaagh! It's a ghost!' he yelled as he turned and ran for his life, scrambling over a stile in his path.

Hack didn't come back the next day, and Alfie settled down to enjoy the rest of his holiday with interruption. But after two more busy days at the farm, Alfie decided to go back to the station. After all he was a *railway cat*, not a farmcat. He was sure Fred could not carry on much longer without him.

He would go home tomorrow.

4

Alfie the Train Driver

Hack was not at all pleased to have Alfie back on duty. 'Oh, here's old Big Head,' he said sarcastically. 'We're in for more trouble.'

'You mean, *you* will be in for trouble if you don't give Alfie the respect due to him,' warned Fred.

Alfie rubbed his cheek against Fred's left trouser leg, purring loudly.

'Showing off, as usual . . .' muttered Hack.

'Once and for all,' warned Fred. 'You will both behave or you'll be sacked. Make up your minds.'

'Oh well,' said Hack. 'I suppose we could try. Are you willing to make and effort to be – er – friends, Alfie?'

Alfie stopped cleaning himself. 'Miaow!' he replied. I'll do my best.

And for two days at least all was peaceful at the station.

Fred was very pleased. 'Keep it up. You are both doing fine,' he said.

But Fred's peace was short-lived. It was Hack's afternoon off, and, feeling bored. Alfie decided he would take time off too. He set off for a walk through the village and then along the riverbank. After a short distance he heard music ahead. He hurried on and reached the grounds of a house, with a large garden overlooking the river. Alfie knew the house and the family who lived there. He squeezed through a gap in the hedge and joined the crowd of children and a few adults who were milling about.

A bell rang and then there was silence as a man jumped on to a small platform and announced, 'I declare this fête in aid of our special children's charity is now open. Please give generously. There are plenty of stalls, raffles, refreshments, competitions – you name it, we have it. Not forgetting the train rides, of course.'

Train rides? Alfie was puzzled, but he soon located the train – and the driver. *Hack* in uniform, was at the controls of a miniature steam railway engine. The train carried passengers on a 15-minute trip around the grounds. Alfie sat and watched but he was soon recognised and then surrounded by the children. They were delighted to see their favourite cat.

How Alfie wished he could go on a train trip with them, but Hack wasn't having any of it. He refused to let Alfie board the train. Alfie had nearly given up hope when a boy, well-known to him, asked for two tickets for the next trip. Hack took the money and handed the tickets to the boy, who promptly picked up Alfie and leapt on board.

'Oh, no you don't, my boy!' cried Hack. 'No animals allowed on the train.'

'But I've paid for his ticket,' protested the boy, and he held up the tickets.

'You heard what I said,' cried Hack. 'No animals allowed. Off, Alfie. I shan't tell you again.'

'But it's my *birthday* and I want Alfie to come with me.'

A small crowd had gathered. Everyone glared at Hack.

'Oh, all right,' he gave in at last. 'But mind you behave yourself, Alfie.'

'Miaow! Miaow!' I always behave myself – or nearly always.

The crowd cheered as Hack blew a whistle and the train moved off. Alfie went on the

round trip over and over again. All the children in turn wanted to take him on the train too, and willingly paid for his ticket.

'Alfie's supposed to be on duty at the station,' Hack protested.

But the parents shut him up. 'It's all for charity,' they shouted.

It was all over too quickly for Alfie. It was a long time since he'd had such fun. When Hack left the train to go for a cup of tea, Alfie jumped up to the driver's seat. The children were delighted. 'The railway cat driver,' they shouted.

A newspaper reporter appeared. 'I want to take a picture of this,' he called out to the children. 'Take your seats in the train for a photograph of Alfie and his passengers. Before the other driver comes back.'

Laughing and joking, the children jumped on the train and took their seats. Hack came running over to see what was going on. 'We'll all be in the newspaper tomorrow,' called the children. But Hack was not at all pleased.

At closing time Alfie sat near the exit watching the children depart. Then he decided he'd go for a last walk through the grounds of the house, to the main river. He had once caught a fish there. He might be lucky again. Coming to the river he spotted two boats at anchor.

A light was switched on in the cabin of one boat and Alfie could clearly see somebody inside. It was Hack! Whoever owned the boat must have lent it to Hack, knowing that Mrs Hack had gone on a visit to her mothers for a week. How jolly, thought Alfie.

Alfie kept watch until the light went out. After a few minutes he crept down to the water's edge and leapt lightly on to the boat.

The door of the cabin was slightly ajar and

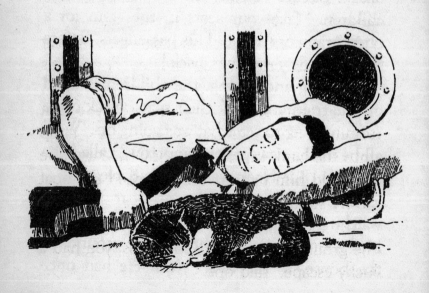

Alfie crawled in. Hack was sound asleep on the bunk, so Alfie curled up alongside him. Soon, he too was fast asleep.

He slept soundly and woke up early. There was no movement from Hack, so he settled down again, but was soon aware of a slight gurgling sound. It must be raining. Alfie then realised he was feeling very cold – and rather wet. He panicked, and sprang up in fright when he realised that water was seeping into the boat. It was slowly sinking. Alfie frantically clawed and clawed at Hack's back until the man woke up and sat upright.

'Whatever–?' he began, 'Oh, it's just you, nuisance.' Hack tried to lie down again.

Alfie howled and was making a hurried exit when Hack cried, 'Help! Help! The boat's sinking!'

There was no-one at hand to help but somehow Hack managed to get out and jump onto the bank in time. He took hold of Alfie and held him tight as they watched the boat slowly sinking.

Just then, two men who were camping in the grounds appeared. 'Goodness, you had a lucky escape,' said one.

'Another minute and you would have sunk along with that boat,' agreed the other.

Hack gulped. 'All thanks to Alfie,' he gasped. 'He's the best railway cat in the country.'

Alfie nearly fell into the river in shock. He never dreamt he'd hear such praise – and from Hack of all people!

Later on, back at the station, Fred listened to Hack's account of the night's adventure.

'Well, well,' said Fred, smiling. 'So Alfie's a hero, is he?'

'He certainly is,' said Hack, 'but I'll still have to . . .' he hesitated.

'Still have to what?' asked Fred.

'Nothing,' said Hack, grinning.

Alfie rolled over on his back. He knew that life without Hack would be no fun at all.

5

Diamond Rescue

One starry night Alfie lay on a bench on the main platform, looking up at the sky. Was there really a man on the moon? he thought.

He felt drowsy and was dropping off to sleep when he was aroused by a sound of footsteps. Two men dressed in dark clothing were coming on to the platform. One of them carried a plastic bag. Alfie recognised the men. They were part-time employees who worked at the Station Hotel during the summer.

The railway cat was puzzled. There was

no-one on duty at the station – except himself, of course – and no stopping trains until early morning. What were they doing at this time of night? Alfie felt sure that the two men were up to no good. He watched as they looked around cautiously, then crept up to the litter bin hanging on the nearby wall. Alfie had seen the bin being emptied earlier that evening.

'All clear?' whispered the man carrying the bag.

'Well the cat's on duty,' said the other man. 'But he's not likely to report us to the police, is he?'

'No, but are you sure the bin won't be emptied until the day after tomorrow?'

'I've told you, I'm quite sure,' was the impatient reply. 'The rubbish collectors are striking on Wednesday – that's tomorrow – we can put the . . .'

The man's voice fell to a whisper, and Alfie strained to hear the rest. Then he heard, '. . . come here tomorrow night take, out the parcel . . . by Thursday morning we'll be miles away with the loot. Satisfied?'

The accomplice nodded. The parcel was placed in the bin and the men disappeared.

Alfie spent a restless night. He was uneasy. Something was very wrong. Next morning he tried to attract Fred's attention to the bin by sitting below it all morning, miaowing whenever Fred or Hack came within earshot.

Hack began to grumble. 'That cat's getting on my nerves. Can't stand his noise much longer. He's worse than usual this morning.'

For once Fred agreed with him. 'I'll see to him at lunch-time. He looks healthy enough. Ate a good breakfast.'

Alfie remained where he was and settled down to wait. During the morning he overheard some passengers gossiping. There had been a robbery at the Station Hotel and among the stolen items was a valuable diamond necklace, belonging to a foreign diplomat who was visiting the village. All the Staff and guests had been interviewed and a search made.

As Alfie grew more restless, two policemen arrived at the station to question the staff and search for any clues. Ticket office, waiting room, staff room, etc. They looked everywhere, with no result.

Alfie did his best to help. He miaowed constantly until one of the policeman called, 'Whatever is the matter, Alfie?' Are they starving you?'

'Starving him,' cried Hack. 'He's got an appetite like a rhinoceros!'

But Fred looked thoughtful. 'Funny,' he said. 'Alfie has been sitting near that bin all morning, miaowing most of the time.'

'Driving us all dotty,' added Hack.

'That's interesting, Fred,' said the policeman. 'Cats are very intelligent animals. Maybe he's trying to tell us something.'

Alfie rolled over on his back. 'Purr...

purr . . . purr,' he sang. Someone with a bit of sense at last!

'There's obviously something in that bin that Alfie thinks we should see,' continued the policeman. 'When was it last emptied?' he asked Hack.

Last night, as usual, but not tonight because of the one day strike,' Hack told him.

So whatever was put in that bin later last night will still be there this evening,' said the officer. 'Agreed?'

'And we'll be ready to pounce!' shouted Hack.

'*You* won't be ready,' said the policeman, 'because you won't be here, and you will *not* speak to anyone about this. If you do, the punishment will be very severe. Is that understood?'

Hack nodded. 'Promise,' he said, and Alfie miaowed. He knew Hack would keep his word.

'Get a newspaper or something and I'll empty the bin,' instructed the policeman.

Hack ran off and soon returned with a newspaper, which was spread out on the platform. The bin was emptied, out fell a jumble of articles, bits of food, paper

wrappings, cigarette ends – and a small square box wrapped in a paper bag.

There was silence as the box was carefully opened to reveal a diamond necklace! 'Good work Alfie!' cried the policeman. He turned to Fred. 'Not a word about this to anyone, Fred. Are you on duty this evening?' Fred nodded. 'Well, stay on duty as normal. We'll be waiting for the thieves when they return.

And all turned out as the policeman had predicted. That evening four policemen and Fred – and Alfie – hid in the waiting room. From where they were they had a good view of the platform. As was expected, the thieves turned up, and emptied the bin, out fell the little box with the rest of the rubbish. And out ran the watching thief catchers.

A struggle began but the police soon got the upper hand and the men were handcuffed, ready to be taken away.

'Oh dear, the Hotel will be short staffed now.' Laughed Fred.

Alfie was thrilled. He'd never dreamt that *he* would be part of a criminal investigation. When all was quiet, Alfie thought about how exciting it had all been. Life was going to be rather dull after this.

But he was wrong. News soon spread that Alfie had helped stop a crime, and he became a local hero. Alfie was pleased, but Hack was not.

'That cat will be the most arrogant, uppish, conceited, troublesome and—' he began.

'— the most intelligent cat in the whole universe,' finished Fred, smiling.

'Miaow!' cried Alfie. 'It's nice to be appreciated.'

Hack couldn't help grinning. 'I suppose it *would* be pretty dull here without Alfie,' he conceded.

'Best railway cat in the whole world,' said Fred.

'Well I wouldn't go as far as that,' said Hack. 'But . . . well . . . er . . . we couldn't really do without him.'

'Miaow,' said Alfie. 'And I couldn't do without you.'

6

Zara The Fortune Teller

'I'm very pleased to see you two behaving,' remarked Fred to Alfie and Hack one morning. 'Miaow!' said Alfie. I do my best.

'Well, it's only that conceited ca—' began Hack.

'If I hear any more from you this morning I will send you home like a naughty school-boy,' said Fred, winking at Alfie. 'I don't think Mrs Hack will be very pleased to see you.'

Hack muttered something under his breath.

Alfie thought it was time to take a walk. He

set off for the village and joined a small queue at the fish shop.

'Sorry, Alfie, nothing for you this morning,' said the fishmonger.

'Oh, do give him a titbit,' said a customer. He deserves a treat every now and then.'

'That's true,' said the fishmonger, smiling.

Soon Alfie was served a small piece of salmon. A treat indeed.

'Miaow!' 'Miaow!' he sang. Many thanks.

He left the shop and made his way to the village hall where people were preparing for a bazaar in aid of a local children's charity.

There was much activity in the hall. People were coming and going, and setting up stalls. Competitions were being organised, and chairs and tables rearranged. Alfie couldn't stay long. Fred would be wondering where he'd got to. He decided to return to the hall later, for the opening ceremony in the afternoon.

Back at the station Alfie kept out of Hack's way, and in due course slipped away, back to the hall, in time for the local mayor's opening speech.

The mayor thanked the people for coming

along to support the charity by spending money at the bazaar. Then he noticed Alfie in the crowd. 'Even your famous Alfie is here,' he said. 'I'm sure someone will treat him to a saucer of milk and perhaps a sardine or two.'

Everybody laughed and Alfie thought how jolly it was. He wandered through the hall, visiting every stall. Then he came to a door marked ZARA FORTUNE TELLER. Alfie had never met a Fortune Teller and he was intrigued. He sat and waited patiently for the door to open. When it did open the vicar's wife emerged. She was smiling.

Soon another woman came along and knocked on the door. This time Alfie crept in behind her. There was a round table, with a white tablecloth, in the middle of the room. Zara the Fortune Teller was sitting at the table, and she gestured for the woman to sit opposite her. Alfie settled on a chair by the wall thinking that Zara looked familiar. But he couldn't quite place her.

Zara's customer sat and waited to hear what her future held. Alfie listened as Zara told of a happy year ahead, with good health, plenty of money and happy holidays. But soon he began to get bored. He yawned, jumped silently down from his chair, and crept under the tablecloth to investigate. When his nose peeped from under the tablecloth again, he heard a loud scream.

'There's something under the table . . . is it a rat?' the customer cried. She carried on screaming, and backed towards the door, just as it opened and Hack walked in.

'Whatever's going on?' he asked as he held on to the woman.

'She says there's something evil under my chair,' said Zara.

'With piercing eyes and—' began the woman.

'All right just stand back and I'll have a look,' said Hack.

He got down on his knees, looked under the chair and pulled Alfie out.

'I might have guessed it was you, playing up again. What do you mean by disturbing my... I mean, Zara, whilst she is telling fortunes for charity. I—' Hack broke off his sentence, flustered.

Ah! thought Alfie, so Zara is *Mrs Hack* after all, what a turn up!

With a tremendous effort, Alfie broke loose and dashed out of the room, across the hall, and through the exit. The doorman winked at him and opened the door. 'Don't worry, Alfie,' he said. 'Hack will get over it.'

But Hack didn't get over it. Nor did Mrs Hack, who flatly refused to cook for Alfie any more. Good news for the Railway Cat. Still better news was that Fred's wife would now be cooking his breakfasts.

For some days after that Hack refused to speak to Alfie and Alfie hissed whenever Hack came anywhere near him. Fred was exasperated. You two need a lesson in good manners. If you do not mend your ways I'll report you to head office and you'll probably both get the sack.'

One morning when Alfie was half asleep on a bench, he opened his eyes to see Hack staggering towards him, carrying two very heavy suitcases. Alfie also noticed a small patch of

oil right in the Leading Railman's path.

Dangerous things, oil patches, thought Alfie. He jumped down and hurled himself at Hack, who dropped one of the suitcases right on his big toe.

Hack screamed loud enough to be heard half a mile away, as he hopped about, clutching his foot.

'Whatever is the matter now?' shouted Fred as he rushed out of his office.

'It's that cat, getting his own back. Came at me like a hurricane. Ouch! Ouch! Ouch!'

'That's not like Alfie,' said Fred, puzzled.

Then he noticed the oil patch. 'You would have had a very nasty fall if you had slipped up on this.' he said, pointing at it. 'Might have broken your back. You should use a trolley for such heavy cases.

Hack looked humble. 'Good job Alfie was around,' he said. 'He's not such a bad cat. He's just . . .'

'Yes? Just what *is* he then?' said Fred.

'Oh he's just our Alfie.' said Hack.

ABOUT THE AUTHOR

Phyllis Arkle was born and educated in Chester, but since 1959 she has lived in the Thames Valley village of Twyford in Berkshire. She is actively interested in the Women's Institute, and does voluntary work in addition to writing and reading. Her other interests include music and bridge.